VIVIENNE WOODFORD

Holly Jolly Breakdown

STRANDED IN A FESTIVE TOWN, SNARKY ZOE MUST FIX HER HOLIDAY MESS AND HER HEART.

LAW OF ATTRACTION CALENDAR

You're the warmth in my winter,
the spark in my holiday,
and the reason this Christmas finally feels like home.

Holly Jolly Breakdown

Written by Vivienne Woodford

Publisher Law of Attraction Calendar LLC

Cover Design by Sassy Design Studio

Copyright © 2024 Law of Attraction Calendar LLC

Disclaimer
All trademarks and characters mentioned are the property of their respective owners. This book is not endorsed by or affiliated with the owners of these trademarks.
This is a work of fiction. Names, characters, businesses, places, events, and incidents are either the products of the author's imagination or used in a fictitious manner. Any resemblance to actual persons, living or dead, or actual events is purely coincidental. The story, including its characters and plot, is entirely made up and does not intend to depict, describe, or represent any real-life events, individuals, or organizations.
This book is intended solely for entertainment purposes and should not be interpreted as reflecting real-world situations or actions. All opinions, expressions, and scenarios are fictional and do not represent the beliefs, actions, or positions of any real individuals or entities.

Table of Contents

Chapter 1

Goodbye Christmas,

Hello Margaritas in Mexico

Christmas is a conspiracy.

That's right, I said it. I'm not talking about the tinsel, the lights, or even the carolers who seem to pop up like a bad rash every December. No, Christmas itself is a full-blown, joy-infested conspiracy designed to torture people like me - those of us who cringe at the sight of red and green, who'd rather gouge our eyes out with a candy cane than attend one more "ugly sweater" party.

Hi, I'm Zoe. And I hate Christmas.

Now, before you judge me, let me clarify: I'm not the Grinch. I don't sneak into houses and steal gifts or anything. I'm more like the Grinch's sarcastic, over-caffeinated cousin who watches from afar and mutters, "Good luck with that." My disdain for this holiday is a finely tuned machine, a perfect blend of childhood trauma and adult cynicism, lubricated by the occasional snarky blog post. You might have heard of it - *"Zoe vs.*

The World." My blog is where I unleash my inner snark upon the unsuspecting masses, who apparently find my dry, sardonic take on life to be "refreshingly honest" or "hilarious" depending on how much they've had to drink.

So, here's the deal. Christmas was never easy growing up. I had two parents who could barely stand to be in the same room together, fighting over whether the tree should be real or fake as if that was the issue tearing their marriage apart. Then, one year, in the middle of unwrapping yet another re-gifted sweater, my dad decided he'd had enough. And by "enough," I mean he grabbed his coat, walked out the door, and never came back.

Merry Christmas, indeed.

Ever since then, Christmas has been my least favorite time of year. And living in Washington doesn't help. This state has an unhealthy obsession with the holiday, and I'm pretty sure there's a law that says every single storefront must be decked out in twinkle lights by December 1st. Even the coffee shops, my sanctuary, have succumbed, their menus suddenly filled with peppermint-this and gingerbread-that. I don't want a peppermint mocha, Janet. I want my regular coffee, minus the jingle bells, thank you very much.

So, this year, I'm doing something different. I'm taking matters into my own hands. I'm escaping. Yep, that's right. While everyone else is singing "Jingle Bells" and sipping eggnog, I'll be soaking up the sun on a beach in Mexico, sipping margaritas, and pretending Christmas doesn't exist. It's the perfect plan. No, scratch that—it's the *only* plan.

I've even written about it on my blog, much to the horror of my readers who react like I've just suggested swapping Santa's sleigh for a minivan - apparently, Christmas is the one untouchable tradition you're not allowed to mess with. The post is titled *"Why I'm Trading Christmas for Tequila: An Escape Plan for the Holiday-Weary."* I laid it all out: the drive down the coast, the warm sands of Baja California, and the endless supply of cocktails that don't come with a side of festive cheer.

So here I am, packing my suitcase with all the essentials: sunglasses, swimsuits, and a stack of books that have absolutely nothing to do with Christmas. My car, an old, beat-up but reliable classic I've affectionately named "Rusty," is gassed up and ready to go. I've downloaded my road trip playlist, heavy on the classic rock and blissfully light on the holiday jingles.

I can't wait to hit the open road, leave this winter wonderland behind, and finally get some peace and quiet.

The Road to Freedom… Or So I Thought.

I'm not even ten miles out of town when I realize that Christmas has other plans for me.

First, it's the traffic. Of course, everyone and their grandma is out shopping for last-minute gifts, clogging up the roads like a bad holiday fruitcake. I honk my horn in frustration, but it's like shouting into the void, nobody cares. I flip the radio station, searching for something, anything that isn't Christmas-related, but every channel is spewing out holiday tunes like it's the last day of the world. Finally, I settle on some classic rock, cranking up the volume in an attempt to drown out the jolly insanity.

But the universe, it seems, is conspiring against me.

I pass by a car with a giant wreath strapped to the front grill, as if the driver decided that the best way to show their holiday spirit was to turn their vehicle into a mobile piece of tinsel. I try to ignore it, focusing instead on the road ahead, but then I hit a detour. Perfect. I'm rerouted through a small town that looks like Santa threw up all over it. There's a giant, inflatable snowman grinning at me from the town square, and the lampposts are wrapped in garlands like they're auditioning for a Hallmark movie.

Seriously? I just want to get to Mexico. Is that too much to ask?

I grip the steering wheel tighter and mutter under my breath. This is exactly why I'm leaving. I don't need this kind of cheer in my life. I need sunshine, warm sand, and a cocktail that doesn't have a candy cane sticking out of it. But as I finally make my way out of the Christmas Nightmare Town, I realize something else.

The weather is getting worse.

It's snowing - no, it's *blizzarding* - and I can barely see the road in front of me. What is this, a Christmas curse? I'm trying to leave all this behind, but the snow seems determined to follow me. Rusty isn't handling the slick roads well, and I'm starting to regret not getting that tire check before leaving. I slow down, cursing under my breath, as the flakes pile up on my windshield faster than the wipers can clear them.

"Come on, come on," I mutter as if Rusty can hear me. But the old girl is struggling, and I start to wonder if maybe, just maybe, this wasn't such a great idea after all.

I pull over at a rest stop, wiping the fog off the inside of my windshield and taking a deep breath. I'm not turning back, no way. I just need to figure out my next move. I pull out my phone, but of course, there's no signal. I glance around, spotting a tiny diner up ahead, its neon sign flickering in the storm.

"Well, it's not Mexico, but it'll have to do," I mutter, grabbing my coat and bracing myself against the wind.

The diner is a relic from another era, booths with cracked vinyl seats, a jukebox in the corner, and a waitress who looks like she's been serving coffee since the place opened. It's warm inside, at least, and I shed my coat, sliding into a booth by the window. A steaming cup of coffee appears in front of me before I even ask for it, and I nod my thanks.

The diner is nearly empty, save for a couple of truckers at the counter and an old man nursing what looks like a slice of apple pie. I pull out my phone again, hoping to see some bars pop up on the screen, but no luck. The waitress, a cheerful woman with a nametag that reads "Betsy," approaches with a smile.

"Snow's coming down pretty hard out there," she says, pouring me a refill. "You traveling far?"

"Mexico," I say, trying to sound nonchalant, as if I do this sort of thing all the time.

"Mexico?" She raises an eyebrow. "In this weather? You sure about that, honey?"

"Positive." I take a sip of the coffee, which is surprisingly good. "I'm escaping Christmas."

Betsy lets out a hearty laugh, and I can't help but smile a little. "Well, I hate to break it to you, but

Christmas is everywhere. Even down in Mexico, I reckon."

I roll my eyes. "Yeah, well, they can keep it. I'm not a fan."

Betsy nods, as if she's heard it all before. "Well, if you change your mind, we've got a tree out back that needs decorating. Could use an extra pair of hands."

I shudder at the thought. "I'll pass, thanks."

She chuckles and moves on to the next customer, leaving me to my thoughts. I stare out the window at the swirling snow, feeling my resolve waver just a little. But no, I'm doing this. I'm getting out of here, and I'm going to sip margaritas on a beach if it's the last thing I do.

The snow doesn't let up. I sit in the diner for what feels like hours, nursing cup after cup of coffee and avoiding the holiday decorations that seem to multiply every time I blink. There's a tiny Christmas tree in the corner, and someone has strung lights around the jukebox. Even here, in the middle of nowhere, Christmas finds a way to sneak in. I glance at the clock, still no signal, still no break in the storm.

I start to wonder if maybe the universe is trying to tell me something. But then I shake my head, dismissing the thought. No way. This is just a minor setback. I'm not about to let a little snow, and a Christmas conspiracy, stop me from reaching my beachside bliss. I've dealt with worse: family Christmases that would put reality TV drama to shame, awkward office parties with "Secret Santa" gifts that screamed "I forgot until the last minute," and one particularly dreadful holiday season spent listening to my roommate's "Boyfriend's Christmas Hits" playlist on repeat.

I am *not* turning back. I'm committed.

I pay the check and head back to Rusty, who's looking more like a snowdrift than a car at this point. I scrape off the windshield, cursing under my breath as my fingers go numb. The snow shows no signs of stopping, and as I climb back inside, I feel a flicker of doubt. But I shove it down. I've got a goal, and nothing - not even this winter wonderland from hell - is going to stop me.

Rusty groans as I start the engine, and for a moment, I think she might give up on me entirely. But she sputters back to life, and I let out a triumphant laugh. "That's my girl," I say, patting the dashboard like it's a loyal dog. I pull back onto the highway, determined to keep going.

But as the miles crawl by, I start to realize that my escape plan isn't going to be as simple as I thought. The snow is relentless, coming down in heavy, swirling sheets that obscure the road. I grip the wheel, squinting through the windshield, and my mind starts to wander.

I think about what Betsy said, about Christmas being everywhere. I'd like to argue with her, but the truth is, she's not wrong. Christmas *is* everywhere. It's in the jingles that play on every station, in the tacky lawn decorations that light up entire neighborhoods, and in the relentless cheer that permeates every coffee shop, gas station, and diner I pass.

It's like a bad horror movie where the monster just keeps coming back.

Hours later, I find myself driving through yet another small town that looks like it was plucked straight out of a snow globe. The streetlights are strung with garlands, and every shop window is dressed up with wreaths and bows. I spot a Santa ringing a bell on the corner, surrounded by a cluster of children with faces full of wonder and sticky fingers.

I want to scream.

Just as I'm about to speed up and escape this festive nightmare, Rusty starts to sputter. I glance at the gas gauge—nearly empty. Perfect. Just what I needed. Spotting a gas station up ahead, I pull in with a resigned sigh. The attendant, a young guy sporting a Santa hat and an annoyingly sincere smile, steps out to pump my gas.

"Merry Christmas!" he says with a grin that's just a little too bright for my taste.

"Yep, you too," I mumble, hoping he'll just take the hint and keep it to small talk. I lean back in my seat, scrolling through my phone to kill time, but still—no signal. The storm's getting worse, and for the first time, I start to feel genuinely trapped.

When the tank is full, I pay and hit the road again, but the snow is relentless. I'm creeping along at a snail's pace, and it's clear I'm not making it to Mexico tonight, or anytime soon, for that matter. My grand escape is looking less like a tropical getaway and more like an episode of *Survivor: Holiday Edition*.

I see a sign for a motel up ahead, the kind of place that advertises "color TV" like it's a major selling point. It's not the beachside cabana I had in mind, but at this point, I'm ready to admit defeat. I pull into the parking lot, resigned to spending the night in this winter wasteland.

I grab my bag and trudge inside, where the lobby is decked out in, what else? Christmas decorations! A fake tree stands in the corner, its plastic branches weighed down with tacky ornaments, and the front desk is covered in red and green tinsel. I let out a groan, heading to the counter where an elderly woman with a festive sweater that reads "Santa's Little Helper" is waiting.

"Checking in?" she asks, her eyes twinkling.

"Yes, please. Just for the night," I say, though we both know I'm not going anywhere until this storm lets up.

She hands me a key, and I make my way to my room, trying to ignore the Christmas music playing softly through the speakers. As I collapse onto the bed, I pull out my laptop, figuring I might as well document this disaster.

"Christmas vs. Zoe: Round 1- The Snowpocalypse," I type, the words flowing faster than I expected. I let my sarcasm spill out onto the page, detailing every frustrating, snow-filled moment of my failed escape. I write about the detours, the wreath-wearing cars, the diner full of festive cheer, and my overwhelming need to get away from it all.

But as I write, something strange happens. My tone softens, just a little. I find myself laughing at the absurdity of it all, even if it's still mixed with plenty of eye-rolls. I close the laptop, feeling a little lighter, if only for a moment.

I stare at the ceiling, listening to the muffled sounds of holiday cheer seeping through the thin walls. It's not what I wanted, not even close. But maybe it's what I need. I pull out my phone and scroll through the pictures I've taken so far; the blurry ones of snow-covered roads, the accidental shot of Santa at the gas station, the neon diner sign flickering in the storm.

It's not Mexico. It's not margaritas on the beach. But it's something.

I grab my laptop again, typing up a new post. *"Christmas Crash: Sometimes You Can't Outrun a Holiday"*. I write about the unexpected detours, the snowstorm that's grounded my plans, and how sometimes the universe has a way of forcing you to confront the things you've been running from. I don't get too deep, but it's enough to feel like I've faced something.

I shut my laptop, and let myself relax. Maybe I won't make it to Mexico, but that doesn't mean I can't find my own way to survive this holiday season. I glance out the window, watching as the snow continues to fall, and I feel a strange sense of calm wash over me.

It's not perfect. It's not the escape I planned. But maybe, just maybe, it's okay.

I pull the covers up, settling in for a night in this kitschy, snowbound motel. Tomorrow's a new day, and who knows? Maybe there's still a way to make this Christmas bearable, if not entirely margarita-free.

And if not, well… I've still got tequila in the trunk.

Chapter 2

Breakdown Blues

in the Land of Holiday Overkill

I wake up the next morning feeling unreasonably optimistic, which is unlike me. The storm has finally let up, and a pale winter sun peeks through the gray clouds, casting a faint glow over everything. I peek out of the motel window, and, to my relief, the world outside looks driveable. The snow is still thick, but it's not coming down anymore, and I can see the highway leading me south, away from this winter wonderland. Today, I'm finally getting out of here.

I throw on some clothes, grab my bag, and head out to Rusty, who's looking more like a half-buried relic than my trusty escape vehicle. But I'm determined. I've got sunshine and tequila on my mind, and nothing's going to stand in my way. I crank up the engine, and Rusty roars to life, her steady rumble reassuring me that today's the day I get back on track.

I hit the road, blasting my "Escape Christmas" playlist, avoiding anything resembling a holiday jingle. For the first time in days, I feel good. Really good! Mexico is within reach, and with each mile, I can practically taste the margaritas. The snow thins out as I drive, and I catch glimpses of the ocean far off to my right. This is what freedom feels like.

But then I see it.

A small town pops up in the distance, looking like it's been lifted straight from a holiday postcard. There's a giant "Welcome to Evergreen Village" sign at the entrance, complete with a smiling Santa and a pair of waving reindeer. The town itself is aggressively, violently festive; like the North Pole threw up on it. Every building is dressed in red and green, garlands hang from streetlamps, and the sidewalks are dusted with fake snow because apparently, the real stuff wasn't enough.

I consider speeding right through, but traffic slows me down to a crawl, forcing me to take in every painfully cheerful detail. There are Christmas markets, toy shops with animatronic elves in the windows, and, because this town has no chill whatsoever, a Santa's workshop complete with a real-life Santa waving at passersby. Kids are lined up outside, their parents snapping photos like this is the happiest place on earth.

I roll my eyes so hard I nearly sprain something.

Just as I'm about to make it past this holiday nightmare, Rusty starts to cough and sputter. The dashboard lights up like a well-lit Christmas tree, and the engine lets out a wheeze that makes my heart sink.

"You've got to be kidding me."

I manage to coast to a stop right in front of an over-the-top Christmas store called "The North Pole Emporium," complete with a mechanical snowman that waves and sings "Frosty the Snowman" on repeat. I'm stranded in the last place on earth I want to be, and the irony is not lost on me. I pop the hood and stare blankly at the engine, as if my intense glare alone could magically fix it. Spoiler alert: it doesn't.

With no other options, I dig my phone out of my pocket, still hoping for a miracle signal, but of course, I'm in a festive dead zone. I spot a tiny repair shop down the street, "Bob's Auto Repair" in faded letters with a wreath hanging crookedly on the door, and I make my way over, praying that Bob, whoever he is, can get me back on the road before I choke on all this holiday spirit.

The garage smells like motor oil and pine-scented air fresheners, because why not? Bob himself, an older guy with a belly that suggests he enjoys Christmas cookies all year long, is under a car, tinkering away. He doesn't look up as I approach, just grunts in acknowledgment.

"Morning. What can I do for ya?" he asks, wiping his hands on a grease-stained rag while he craws out from underneath the car.

I explain my predicament, and he nods thoughtfully, rubbing his chin as if he's considering something very important. "I'll have Jimmy bring it in, take a look. Might take a bit, though. We're pretty busy."

Busy? Really? In Santa's Village?

"How long is 'a bit'?" I ask, trying to keep the impatience out of my voice.

"Hard to say. Could be a day, maybe two. Depends on the parts," Bob says with a shrug, as if my entire plan to escape Christmas isn't hanging in the balance.

I force a tight smile. "Right. Thanks."

Bob gives me a sympathetic nod that does nothing to ease my growing frustration, and I slink back to the sidewalk, watching as Jimmy, a guy who looks like he moonlights as an elf, tows Rusty into the garage. I'm officially stuck, and it's beginning to feel like Christmas is holding me hostage.

With Rusty out of commission and no clear way to escape, I start scanning the town for a place to stay. Evergreen Village is like a theme park, with every building either trying to sell me a Santa figurine or some kind of holiday-themed pastry. I spot a quaint, historic-looking inn at the end of the main street, its sign cheerfully proclaiming it "The Holly Jolly Inn." It's decked out in wreaths, twinkling lights, and a giant inflatable Santa perched on the roof. Of course.

I head inside, the jingle of sleigh bells announcing my arrival. The lobby is like stepping into a Christmas explosion: a towering tree in the corner, stockings hung by the fake fireplace, and garlands everywhere. The air smells like cinnamon and pine, and I can practically hear the inn whispering, "Welcome, Zoe. Enjoy your festive nightmare."

Behind the front desk is a man who looks like he walked straight out of a holiday commercial. Tall, with broad shoulders, warm eyes, and a flannel shirt that screams "I bake cookies and chop wood," he greets me with a smile that could thaw the iciest heart. Unfortunately for him, mine is still very much frozen.

"Welcome to The Holly Jolly Inn! I'm Ben, the owner. You look like you've had a rough morning. Can I get you some hot cocoa?"

He says it with such genuine warmth that I almost feel bad for snapping, but I'm on edge, and the holiday overload isn't helping. "Got anything stronger?"

Ben laughs, unfazed. "There's mulled wine at the bar, but trust me, our cocoa's the best in town."

I glance around, taking in the over-the-top décor. "The competition must be fierce."

Ben doesn't miss a beat. "You'd be surprised."

I sigh, defeated by cheerfulness. "I need a room. My car's in the shop, and apparently, I'm stuck here."

Ben nods sympathetically. "Happens more often than you'd think. But don't worry, Bob and Jimmy are the best—if anyone can get you back on the road, it's those two. In the meantime, we've got a room ready for you. First night's on the house; it's just our way of keeping the holiday spirit alive."

I force a smile, though it probably looks more like a grimace. "Lucky me."

Ben leads me up the stairs, past garland-wrapped banisters and holiday-themed paintings that look like they've been commissioned by Santa himself. He opens the door to my room, and it's exactly what I feared: a Christmas nightmare. The bedspread is covered in reindeer prints, there's a mini tree on the dresser, and twinkle lights frame the windows.

"It's… a lot," I say, trying to sound polite. Ben chuckles.

"It's not for everyone, but we like to go all out. If you need anything, just let me know."

"Yeah, thanks," I mumble, throwing my bag on the bed. Ben gives me one last smile before closing the door, leaving me alone with my overly festive prison.

I flop onto the bed and stare at the ceiling, which is painted with, of course, snowflakes. I pull out my laptop, needing to vent. *"Trapped in Santa's Village: My Holiday Hostage Situation"* feels like the perfect title, and I let the words flow. I detail every absurd, over-the-top aspect of Evergreen Village and its relentless commitment to holiday cheer, punctuating each description with enough sarcasm to fill a stocking.

I finish the post, feeling a little better. I'm stuck, sure, but at least I can still poke fun at the madness. And if Ben's mulled wine is as good as his hot cocoa, I might just survive this holiday hostage situation.

For now.

Chapter 3

The Innmate's Tale:

Stuck in Christmas Town

Against My Will

Being stuck in Christmas Town is like getting lost in a never-ending holiday special, the kind where everyone's too cheerful, the snow is too sparkly, and there's not a single person rolling their eyes. It's my third day in Evergreen, and I've run out of synonyms for "tacky" in my blog drafts. I wander down Main Street, dodging happy families and random groups of people who spontaneously burst into carols like we're in some kind of twisted musical.

I snap pictures of anything that screams over-the-top Christmas; a shop window with a train set that loops around a mountain of stuffed reindeer, a group of kids gleefully decorating the sidewalk into a never-ending game of Christmas hopscotch out of chalk, and a Santa who seems to wave at me every time I pass, like he's mocking my misery. I'm determined to capture every cringe-worthy detail, hoping my readers will appreciate my suffering.

I'm hiding out at Mrs. Claus's Kitchen, typing furiously and fueling up on coffee that's as bitter as my mood, when Ben suddenly appears with a tray of cookies shaped like reindeer. He drops into the seat across from me with that annoyingly friendly grin that I've come to expect.

"Good morning! You look busy."

"Just documenting the local insanity," I say, gesturing to my laptop screen. "I've already covered the animatronic reindeer, the holiday light overdose, and how this entire town might be clinically addicted to tinsel."

Ben laughs, unbothered. "Sounds like you're really getting into the spirit."

"Oh, I'm definitely getting into something," I quip, then take a sip of coffee. "Speaking of spirit, please tell me my car's ready so I can escape this nightmare."

Ben's smile falters just a little, and I brace myself. "About that… I just talked to Bob. Turns out, the repairs are gonna take a bit longer than he thought."

"How much longer?" I ask, already dreading the answer.

"A few more days," Ben says, trying to sound casual, like he's just told me they're out of my favorite cereal and not that I'm stuck in Candy Cane Prison for the foreseeable future.

I blink at him, letting the disappointment seep in. "A few more days? Ben, it was supposed to be today. I've already mentally crossed the border into Mexico."

"Yeah, I know," he says, offering a sheepish shrug. "Bob's trying, but it's the holidays. Parts take longer to get here, and Jimmy's down with the flu."

I groan, slumping back in my chair. "Great. Just my luck. Trapped in a snow globe with no exit."

Ben gives me that annoyingly cheerful smile, the kind that says everything's just a festive adventure waiting to happen. "Hey, it's not the worst place to be stuck. Evergreen has its perks. And who knows? Maybe you'll find something you actually like. I was just about to go rummaging through the inn's attic for some old decorations. Care to join? It's practically a treasure hunt."

I raise an eyebrow, sipping my coffee. "You're asking me to voluntarily go deeper into Christmas? What's next, you gonna dress me up as Mrs. Claus?"

Ben laughs. "Not unless you want to. But seriously, it's not just decorations up there. There's all kinds of stuff. Could be fun!"

I consider saying no, but I'm already getting cabin fever, and the thought of rummaging through a dusty attic actually sounds like a welcome break from the relentless holiday cheer. Plus, there's something about Ben's optimism that's hard to completely brush off.

"Fine," I say, shrugging like I'm doing him a massive favor. "But if there are spiders, you're on your own."

We make our way back to the inn, trudging through the cold while Ben points out little things around town; a new sign someone's painted, the Christmas decoration contest winners from last year; the lady who is selling Christmas wreaths in all colors and styles. It's all charming in a small-town, everything's-a-big-deal kind of way. Ben talks about the town like he's narrating a quaint documentary, and despite myself, I'm listening.

When we get back to the inn, Ben grabs a flashlight and a key from the front desk. He leads me up a creaky staircase to a door at the end of the hall, which opens to reveal the kind of attic that every horror movie is made of: dark, dusty, and full of who-knows-what lurking in the shadows.

"You sure you know what you're getting into?" I tease as we climb up the ladder.

Ben smirks, shining the flashlight around. "I think I can handle it. But if we see any rats, you're on distraction duty."

"Noted," I say, stepping into the attic and immediately regretting every life choice that's led me here. It's a maze of boxes, old furniture, and random holiday décor piled in precarious stacks. There's an eerie charm to it, like it's frozen in time.

Ben rummages through a box labeled "Vintage Christmas" and pulls out an ancient-looking Santa with one eye missing. He holds it up with a bemused grin. "Think this will scare the kids?"

"Oh, definitely," I snort. "Nothing says 'Merry Christmas' like Cyclops Santa."

We keep digging, finding more treasures: a tangled mess of old lights that might actually be a fire hazard, a set of reindeer antlers that look like they've seen better days, and an oversized elf costume that I swear is staring at me from the corner.

Ben picks up a photo album covered in glitter and dust, flipping it open. "Hey, look at this. Christmas here back in the 80s. Talk about some bad sweater choices."

I peek over his shoulder, unable to suppress my grin. The pictures are a mix of awkward group shots, kids sitting on a particularly grumpy Santa's lap, and what looks like a very festive, very chaotic holiday party in the inn's lobby. There's a faded photo of a young couple dancing by the fireplace, garlands overhead and smiles that practically glow.

"Is that you?" I ask, pointing at a picture of a boy with a toothy grin and eyes that are unmistakably Ben's.

Ben nods, laughing. "Yep, that's me. My parents used to run the inn. This place was always the center of Christmas in town. Guess it kind of stuck with me."

There's a fondness in his voice, and for a moment, I see Ben differently. Not just as the perpetually cheerful innkeeper, but as someone who's built his life around this little slice of holiday magic. It's sweet, in a completely sappy, Ben-like way.

I pick up a dusty ornament shaped like a mini Ferris wheel, its colors faded and a little chipped. "This looks ancient. Why keep all this stuff?"

Ben shrugs. "Memories, I guess. It's a way of keeping the past alive. Plus, you never know when you'll need a one-eyed Santa to liven things up."

I roll my eyes, but there's a smile sneaking onto my face. "You really are Mr. Christmas, aren't you?"

"Guilty as charged," he says, holding up a strand of tinsel like it's a prized possession. "But hey, everyone needs a little magic now and then. Even Grinches."

We keep digging, the attic turning into a treasure hunt of nostalgia and oddities. Ben's stories flow easily; about past guests, holiday mishaps, and the time his dad dressed up as Santa and got stuck in the chimney. I add my sarcastic commentary where appropriate, but mostly, I'm just enjoying the easy banter.

It's ridiculous, really. I'm stuck in a tiny attic, rummaging through Christmas past with a guy who's one candy cane away from being Santa himself. But for the first time since I got stranded in this town, I don't mind. It's just me, Ben, and a heap of old memories that somehow feel lighter in his company.

Maybe it's the attic dust making me soft. Or maybe, just maybe, there's a little room for this Christmas nonsense after all.

But I'll never admit it.

Chapter 4

When a Grinch Gets Roped into Christmas Cheer

When Ben suggested joining a baking contest at the inn, I should have known that agreeing was the first of many mistakes. It started innocently enough with him saying, "It's just a friendly little competition, no pressure." But, of course, I learned quickly that nothing is ever that simple when Ben is involved. Now I find myself standing in the inn's bustling kitchen, surrounded by mixing bowls, cookie cutters, and enough holiday-themed sprinkles to make a dentist cry.

"Just think of it as a stress-free way to pass the time," Ben had said with his infuriatingly charming smile. "You'll have fun, I promise."

Fun. Sure. Because my idea of fun is battling dough that refuses to cooperate while surrounded by half the town's eager bakers who seem to be auditioning for their own cooking show. But somehow, his cheerfulness had gotten to me, and now here I am, apron on, flour in my hair, and a sinking feeling that this is going to go spectacularly wrong.

I stare down at the recipe card in front of me: "Classic Christmas Sugar Cookies." It sounds easy enough, but I know better. I can already picture the cookies coming out of the oven looking less like snowflakes and more like abstract art. Meanwhile, Ben is at the station next to me, humming a Christmas tune while expertly measuring ingredients. He's moving like he's done this a thousand times; calm, collected, and, annoyingly, really good at it.

"You look like you're planning a baking revolution," Ben says, glancing over at my scattered ingredients. "Everything okay over there?"

"Living the dream," I say, trying to scrape butter that's still rock-solid into the bowl. "I'm one step away from calling in a pastry exorcist."

Ben chuckles, his eyes twinkling. "Need any help?"

"Nope," I insist, stabbing at the butter like it's offended me personally. "I've got this."

I'm lying, of course. Baking is not my forte. My talents lie more in the realm of snarky blog posts and avoiding festive activities, not creating picture-perfect cookies. Still, I'm determined not to let Ben, or the universe, see me flounder. I toss some sugar into the bowl with an impressive amount of confidence for someone who's already missed a step or two.

The kitchen is buzzing with activity. Families and couples are chatting, laughing, and skillfully decorating cookies that look ready for the cover of a holiday magazine. Meanwhile, I'm staring at my lump of dough, which has somehow taken on the consistency of cement. I start to mix it with a wooden spoon, but it's like trying to stir a bowl of concrete.

"How's it going, Zoe?" Ben asks, casually leaning against the counter, effortlessly rolling out his perfectly smooth dough. "Need a hand?"

I glare at him, then down at my dough. "Oh, no. I'm just fine. This is how it's supposed to look."

Ben tilts his head, hiding a smile. "Sure it is. Want some tips?"

I huff, still struggling to make the dough behave. "I'm just embracing my inner artist. Maybe this is a new form of cookie sculpture."

Ben watches me with amusement as I wrestle with the dough, which stubbornly clings to the spoon like it's staging a protest. He reaches over, his hand brushing mine as he takes the spoon and starts to work the dough with the finesse of someone who clearly knows what he's doing.

"Here, you've just got to give it a little elbow grease," he says, his voice low and reassuring.

I feel a flutter in my chest that has nothing to do with baking and everything to do with how close Ben is. I try to focus on the task at hand, but his presence is distracting in the worst (and best) way. He's too charming, too competent, and suddenly this whole baking disaster feels a little more tolerable.

After a few minutes, the dough is finally behaving, and I'm able to roll it out. I grab a star-shaped cookie cutter and press it into the dough, feeling a small victory as the shape comes out more or less intact.

"See? Not so hard," Ben says, nudging my shoulder playfully. "You've got this."

I scoff, but it's half-hearted. "Yeah, yeah. Don't get too confident in my skills just yet."

With the cookies finally cut out and arranged on the baking sheet, I slide them into the oven and set the timer.

I lean against the counter, trying to look like I have this whole thing under control, but the truth is, I'm already mentally preparing myself for disaster.

Ben's cookies, of course, are perfect. They're golden brown, evenly shaped, and cooling on a wire rack like something out of a Christmas catalog. Meanwhile, I'm anxiously watching my oven, expecting smoke to start pouring out at any moment.

The timer dings, and I carefully open the oven, bracing myself. To my surprise, the cookies are… not terrible. They're a little misshapen, sure, and one of them looks like it's trying to run away, but they're not burnt. I let out a breath.

Ben glances over and gives me an encouraging nod. "Hey, those look great. Told you, you could do it."

"Don't get too excited," I say, but I'm secretly relieved. "The decorating part is where it all goes south."

We set up at the decorating station, which is an explosion of icing tubes, colored sugars, and candy bits. Ben starts effortlessly piping designs onto his cookies, while I attempt to do the same, but with far less finesse. My first cookie ends up with what I can only describe as "abstract holiday art." The snowflake looks more like it's melting, and the tree might be mistaken for a green blob in a different context.

"Creative," Ben says, his eyes twinkling as he admires my work. "Definitely one-of-a-kind."

"Oh, it's avant-garde," I say, trying to play it off. "You wouldn't understand."

Ben laughs, and I can't help but laugh with him. There's something undeniably fun about this, even if my cookies look like they've been through a windstorm. We end up working side by side, decorating cookies with more laughter than skill. I'm elbow-deep in green icing when Ben decides to show off, crafting a perfect reindeer with delicate antlers.

"Okay, show-off," I say, shaking my head. "You've clearly done this before."

"A few times," he admits, and there's a softness to his tone. "My mom and I used to bake together every Christmas. It's kind of a tradition."

I glance at him, caught off guard by the sincerity in his voice. It's the first time I've seen Ben without his usual joking demeanor, and for a moment, the playful banter falls away. He looks… well, sweet. And not just because he's holding a cookie.

Before I can respond, a group of kids rushes into the kitchen, giggling and chattering loudly. They're pointing up at something, and when I look, my heart drops.

Mistletoe. Right above us. Because of course it is.

"Oh, you've got to be kidding me," I mutter, feeling my cheeks flush. The kids start chanting, "Kiss! Kiss! Kiss!" like they've been waiting for this moment all day.

Ben glances at me, and I can see the amusement in his eyes, but there's also something else, a flicker of uncertainty, like he's not sure if this is a joke or something more. He steps a little closer, his expression softening.

"Guess we're caught," he says, his voice low and teasing.

I swallow, trying to play it cool. "Yeah, guess so."

We're standing inches apart now, and I can feel the tension building between us, thick enough to cut with a cookie cutter. It's one of those moments that feels frozen in time, and for a split second, I forget where we are, surrounded by flour, icing, and a bunch of nosy kids. All

I can think about is Ben, and how easy it would be to just lean in…

But before anything happens, a crash breaks the spell. One of the kids, trying to get a better view of our impending kiss, has knocked over the table, sending cookies flying in every direction. The spell is broken, and Ben and I both step back, laughing awkwardly as we rush to clean up the mess.

"Saved by the chaos," I say, bending down to pick up the fallen cookies.

Ben grins, still a little breathless. "Yeah. Or cursed by it."

We gather the cookies and set them back on the tray, and the kids eventually scatter, bored now that the show's over. I steal a glance at Ben, wondering what he's thinking, but he just smiles, and it's hard to tell if he's as flustered as I am.

As the contest judging begins, the bakers present their creations with pride. There are intricately decorated snowflakes, perfectly piped reindeer, and cookies so beautiful they look almost too good to eat. Then there are mine, which are… well, unique. I plate them with a flourish, deciding to own my messy creations.

"'Most Artistic Disaster' should definitely be a category," I say to Ben as I set the plate down.

"I'd vote for you," he says, nudging me playfully. "You put a lot of heart into those."

"Or a lot of stress," I joke, but his words make me smile.

The judges, mostly a mix of inn guests and townsfolk, sample each batch, murmuring their approvals. When they get to mine, I hold my breath, waiting for the inevitable critique. But instead, they smile, and one of the judges even chuckles.

"These have… character," he says diplomatically.

"Just like the baker," Ben adds, and I shoot him a look, but I'm secretly touched.

In the end, I don't win any official prize, but they do give me a special ribbon for "Most Enthusiastic Effort," which feels like a backhanded compliment but also kind of perfect. Ben's cookies take second place, and he feigns disappointment, but I can tell he's just happy to have participated.

As we pack up, Ben hands me one of my own cookies, slightly broken but still intact. "Not bad for a Grinch."

"Not bad at all," I admit, feeling the warmth of the moment settle in. We share a look, the kind that says more than words can, and for once, I let myself just enjoy it. Maybe being stuck here isn't so bad after all.

Or maybe, it's just Ben.

Chapter 5

Fireside Confessions

The inn's kitchen is finally winding down from the chaotic mess of the baking contest, with the last few guests trickling out and congratulating each other on their confectionery masterpieces. The air is filled with the sweet scents of sugar, cinnamon, and freshly baked cookies, mingling together like a warm holiday hug. I'm trying to shake off the weird feeling from earlier, that almost-kiss under the mistletoe with Ben that had my heart doing all sorts of somersaults.

I thought I'd be relieved to get out of the kitchen, but I can't stop replaying the moment in my mind; the way Ben's eyes softened, the way his smile hinted at something more, the way my heart leaped before I could stop it. I didn't expect this, any of it. I came to this town planning to dodge Christmas cheer, not to get tangled up in it, or in him.

Just as I'm contemplating a quiet, solo retreat to my room, Ben finds me in the inn's lobby. He's still wearing that easy smile of his, but there's a new flicker of something in his eyes that I can't quite place. He looks tired, maybe a little pensive, and for a second, I wonder if he's still thinking about the almost-kiss, too.

"Hey, you okay?" he asks, leaning casually against the doorframe. "You seem a little lost in thought."

I blink, snapping out of my reverie. "Oh, yeah, just… decompressing from the cookie war."

He chuckles softly. "Yeah, that was a bit more intense than I expected. But you did great, really."

I roll my eyes, but it's more playful than annoyed. "Yeah, nothing says 'great' like 'Most Enthusiastic Effort.'" I twirl the little red ribbon between my fingers, and Ben laughs, his grin tugging at my nerves in all the right ways.

"Hey, we're having a bonfire down by the square tonight," he says, his voice dropping slightly. "Thought you might want to join. It's kind of a tradition around here, a way to wind down after a busy day. Plus, you might actually enjoy it."

I hesitate, not because I don't want to go, but because every time I spend more time with Ben, things feel a little more complicated. Still, something about the idea of a warm fire and some fresh air sounds like exactly what I need.

"Sure," I say, shrugging like it's no big deal. "Why not? Could use a little more fresh air after all the powdered sugar I inhaled."

Ben grins, and we head out together, making our way through the crisp night air toward the village square.

When we arrive at the square, the bonfire is already roaring, a flickering glow that casts warm light on the gathering of villagers, young and old. They're bundled up in scarves and hats, sharing laughter and hot drinks, all huddled close to the crackling flames. There's a feeling of community here, the kind that I've always scoffed at in theory but can't help but admire in person.

Ben nudges me gently, leading me to a spot near the fire where a few empty logs are set up as makeshift benches. He hands me a steaming cup of mulled cider from a nearby table, and I take it gratefully, wrapping my hands around the mug to keep warm.

"So, what's the deal with this bonfire?" I ask, blowing on my cider to cool it down. "Seems like everyone's been doing this forever."

Ben gazes into the fire, a soft smile playing on his lips. "Yeah, it's been around for a while. My parents started it, actually. They wanted a way for everyone to gather, especially on these cold nights. They always said it was to keep everyone warm, but really, it was more about sharing the moment."

He pauses, staring into the flames with a fondness that tells me this is more than just an evening event; it's a piece of his family's history.

We sit in comfortable silence for a while, watching the flames lick and curl, the wood popping and crackling as it burns. Around us, people are chatting and laughing, and the whole scene feels oddly cozy, like a painting I'd never imagine myself in. I find my gaze drifting back to Ben, who's staring into the fire with a faraway look, like he's a million miles away.

"Hey," I say softly, nudging him with my elbow. "What's going on in that head of yours?"

He hesitates for a moment, like he's weighing his words carefully. "I was just… thinking about my parents," he finally says. "They used to love nights like this. My mom would always bake these ridiculous pies that never turned out quite right, but no one cared. It was more about being together."

I nod, taking another sip of cider. "Sounds like they really loved Christmas."

"They did," Ben says, his voice growing softer, more reflective. "It was kind of their thing. They made every holiday feel like this big, magical event. And then I met Sarah, and she… well, she just fit right into it all. She loved this time of year as much as they did."

I freeze, hearing the unfamiliar name, and there's a sudden weight in Ben's words that pulls my attention away from the fire and straight to him.

"Sarah?" I ask, my voice gentle.

Ben nods, staring into his cup. "Yeah. She was my wife. We met right here in Evergreen. She was... everything, really. Loved this town, loved Christmas, and somehow loved me even more. We got married right here in the square, under the Christmas lights."

There's a rawness in his tone, and for a moment, I feel like I'm intruding on something deeply private. But Ben keeps talking, like he's been holding this story inside for a long time and finally needs to let it out.

"She was the one who really made Christmas feel like home," he continues, his voice thick with emotion. "But five years ago… there was an accident. She was driving back from her parents' place, just a few days before Christmas, and… it was icy, and she lost control."

He stops, swallowing hard, and I can see the pain etched in his expression, even through the flickering shadows. I reach out instinctively, placing a hand on his arm, and he looks up, his eyes reflecting the firelight and something deeper—grief, love, and the weight of memories that never fade.

"Ben, I'm so sorry," I say, and I mean it. I don't know what else to say, and for once, my sarcasm feels useless and small.

Ben nods, forcing a small smile. "Thanks. It's been… hard, you know? But this place, these traditions… they keep me going. She loved this town, and I feel like keeping these things alive is my way of keeping her close."

We sit in silence, the fire crackling softly between us. I can't help but admire Ben's strength, his ability to find joy in the little things even when life has dealt him such a heavy blow. And suddenly, his unwavering cheerfulness makes perfect sense. It's not just about Christmas or tradition; it's about holding on to the things that remind him of the people he's lost.

"You're a lot stronger than you let on," I say quietly, my eyes meeting his. "It's hard to keep that kind of light going after everything."

Ben's smile is sad but genuine. "You learn to carry it. And sometimes, it helps to have people around who don't mind sharing the weight."

I don't know what to say to that, so I just squeeze his arm, offering the silent comfort of being there. It's a strange, delicate moment, both heavy and light, filled with unspoken understanding. I've always been good at keeping my distance, but sitting here with Ben, sharing stories under the stars, I feel like I'm finally starting to let my guard down.

As we continue to talk, a gentle snowfall begins to drift down, tiny flakes catching the light of the fire as they dance around us. It's unexpected, beautiful, and the entire village square is transformed into a soft, glowing wonderland. I pull my coat tighter, the chill creeping in, and Ben shifts closer, our shoulders brushing.

"Looks like the weather had other plans," Ben says, his breath visible in the cool night air. "Guess it's not a bonfire without a little snow."

I laugh softly. "Yeah, I didn't picture it being so… picturesque. I feel like we're trapped in a snow globe."

"Not a bad place to be," he says, nudging me gently. "At least we're in it together."

I glance up at him, feeling that same pull from earlier in the kitchen. It's not just the heat of the fire warming me now; it's the quiet closeness, the shared space that feels surprisingly intimate. The snow continues to fall around us, and there's a peace in the air that I haven't felt in a long time.

"Thanks for sharing all that with me," I say, my voice barely above a whisper. "You didn't have to."

Ben meets my gaze, his eyes soft and warm. "I wanted to. I don't really talk about her much, but… I think she'd like you."

I feel my heart stutter, the words catching me off guard. "You think so?"

He nods, and there's a sincerity in his smile that makes my chest ache. "Yeah. She always had a soft spot for people who were a little rough around the edges."

I can't help but smile, touched in a way I didn't expect. "Sounds like my kind of person."

Ben shifts a little closer, our knees nearly touching, and I feel the warmth of his presence wash over me. The snow is falling thicker now, swirling gently around us, and I lean into the moment, letting go of all the reasons I've kept myself so guarded.

"You know, I came here planning to avoid all this," I admit, gesturing to the town, the bonfire, the whole scene. "Christmas, the small-town thing, all of it. But… I don't know. I think I'm starting to get it."

Ben's smile widens, a soft, genuine expression that makes my heart flutter. "Sometimes, it just takes the right people to help you see things differently."

We sit there for a long moment, the world around us quiet and still except for the soft whisper of snow and the crackling fire. There's no noise, no pressure—just two people sharing a quiet, unexpected connection that feels as delicate and perfect as the snowflakes landing on our shoulders.

Ben's fingers trace a delicate path through my hair, brushing away the lone snowflake that's landed there, but his touch lingers, soft and warm against the chill of the night. It's such a simple gesture, yet it sends a rush of heat through me, spreading from where his hand rests, all the way to my racing heart. Our eyes lock, and it's like the whole world narrows down to this one perfect moment; no jokes, no walls, just the two of us being impossibly close. The connection between us pulses, electric and undeniable, something far deeper than friendship and far more intense than I ever allowed myself to imagine.

I feel the magnetic pull drawing me closer, like he's gravity and I'm helpless to resist. His touch is gentle but charged, every brush of his fingers sending sparks of warmth that make my skin tingle. I can see it in his eyes. This shared, unspoken understanding that whatever this is, it's real and raw and more than either of us planned. The space between us shrinks, and all the doubts, all the fears that usually keep me running, seem to dissolve into the snowy night. For the first time, I'm not thinking about what comes next or how this might end. I'm just here, caught in the heat of his gaze, wanting nothing more than to be close to him and lose myself in the moment.

"Zoe," he says softly, his voice low and full of unspoken things.

"Yeah?" I whisper back, feeling the weight of the moment settle in.

But before either of us can say anything more, the village clock chimes, breaking the silence and jolting us back to reality. I pull away slightly, laughing at the absurd timing, and Ben shakes his head, clearly as caught off guard as I am.

"Guess that's our cue," he says, smiling but with a touch of lingering tension.

"Yeah, guess so," I agree, though I can't help but feel a little disappointed.

We stand up, brushing the snow from our coats, and head back toward the inn. The snow continues to fall, blanketing the square in a soft, shimmering layer. Ben walks close beside me, his presence comforting in the cold night, and I can't help but feel that something has shifted between us. It's not just Christmas that's starting to grow on me; it's Ben, with his quiet strength, his stories, and the way he makes me feel like maybe, just maybe, this little town isn't such a bad place to be.

As we reach the inn, Ben pauses at the door, turning to face me. "Thanks for coming tonight. I know this isn't your thing, but... it means a lot."

I smile, feeling the warmth of his words. "Yeah, well, you're kind of hard to say no to."

He laughs softly, and for a moment, it feels like there's so much more to say. But instead, we just share a quiet smile, the kind that says everything without needing to say a word.

"Goodnight, Zoe," Ben says, his voice gentle.

"Goodnight, Ben," I reply, and as I head inside, I can't help but glance back, catching one last look at him standing in the falling snow.

Chapter 6

Cold Feet and Bus Tickets

The morning after the bonfire, I wake up with a heavy sense of disorientation, like I've spent the night dreaming in technicolor and can't quite shake the haze. I stare up at the ceiling, my mind replaying bits and pieces of last night. Ben's voice soft and sincere, sharing stories of his past, the flickering glow of the bonfire, and the unexpected comfort of being close to him under the falling snow.

It's not where I thought I'd be, emotionally or physically. I've spent my whole life building walls, making sure that no one ever gets too close, and here I am, stuck in the cheeriest place on earth, feeling something I can't quite name. Ben's story about Sarah, his late wife, lingers in my mind like a song I can't turn off, and the vulnerability he showed last night feels like a gift I wasn't ready to receive.

I roll out of bed, dragging myself to the window. The world outside is covered in a soft, white blanket, and I watch as kids build snowmen and couples stroll arm-in-arm down Main Street, looking like they've just stepped out of a postcard. I should feel annoyed by it all, but instead, there's this nagging warmth that's hard to ignore.

I came to Evergreen with a plan: avoid Christmas, avoid people, avoid feelings. But somehow, this town, and Ben, have managed to worm their way into my carefully guarded heart. And that scares me more than anything. I can't let myself get too comfortable, too attached. I've been down that road before, and it's never ended well.

I pull on some clothes and head downstairs, determined to shake off the strange mix of emotions bubbling inside me. The inn's dining room is bustling with activity, guests chatting over steaming cups of coffee and plates piled high with pancakes and bacon. I spot Ben at the far end, pouring coffee for a couple of guests with his usual easygoing smile. He looks up as I approach, his eyes lighting up in that annoyingly familiar way that sends a rush of warmth through me.

"Morning, Grinch," he says, teasing as he hands me a cup of coffee. "Sleep okay?"

"Yeah, like a log," I lie, forcing a smile. "How about you?"

He shrugs, leaning against the counter with that effortless charm. "Not bad. Was a good night."

I nod, sipping my coffee and hoping it'll jolt me back to reality. "Yeah, it was… something."

Ben watches me, his smile fading just a touch. "You seem off. Everything okay?"

"Yeah, totally," I say, too quickly. "Just, you know, processing."

He looks at me, really looks at me, and I feel exposed under his gaze, like he can see every thought running through my mind. "I think you're finally starting to like it here," he says, his tone light but with a hint of something deeper. "Evergreen's growing on you."

I flinch at his words, the truth of them hitting a little too close. "Don't get ahead of yourself," I say, trying to sound playful, but my voice comes out sharper than I intended. "I'm just… trying to make the best of being stuck."

Ben's smile falters, and there's a flicker of hurt in his eyes that twists my stomach. "Zoe, it's okay to like it here, you know. To let yourself enjoy it."

I set my cup down a little too hard, the clatter loud enough to draw a few curious glances from the nearby tables. "You don't get it, Ben. I didn't come here to enjoy anything. I came here to get away."

Ben straightens, the easygoing vibe between us evaporating. "Get away from what? Because it seems like you're running more than anything."

His words hit like a sucker punch, and I can't tell if I'm angry at him for saying it or at myself for knowing he's right. "I'm not running," I snap, though even I don't believe it. "I just… I don't belong here. This place, all of this… it's not for me."

Ben watches me, and the disappointment in his eyes stings more than I care to admit. "Maybe it could be, if you'd let it."

I can't do this. Not now, not here. Not when I feel this close to losing control. "I've gotta go," I mumble, turning on my heel before I can see the hurt on his face. I push through the dining room, the noise of the breakfast crowd fading as I rush back to my room, heart pounding in my chest.

I slam the door behind me, leaning against it as I try to catch my breath. Everything feels too close, too intense, and I can't stand the idea of staying here another second longer. I need to get out. I need to escape before I let this place, or Ben, get any closer.

I grab my laptop, fingers flying over the keyboard as I search for bus schedules. My car's still in the shop, and with Bob's perpetually optimistic "a few more days," I can't wait any longer. I scroll through the options, my anxiety spiking with every click. There's a bus that leaves tomorrow morning, early enough that I can slip away without anyone noticing. It'll take me to the next town over, and from there, I can figure out the rest. Mexico, maybe. Anywhere but here.

I book the ticket without thinking twice, the confirmation email popping up like a promise of freedom. I shut the laptop, feeling the immediate rush of relief. I'm leaving. I'll be gone before the sun rises. No goodbyes, no explanations. It's what I'm good at. Cutting ties before they can tighten around me.

But as I sit there, staring at the screen, the relief starts to sour. The thought of leaving Evergreen, of leaving Ben, makes my chest ache in a way that I don't want to examine too closely. I hate that I care, that I've let myself get pulled into this strange little world of snowflakes and bonfires and baking contests. I hate that for a moment, it felt like maybe I could stay.

I push the thoughts aside, stuffing my laptop back into my bag with more force than necessary. I've made my decision. I'm leaving, and that's all there is to it. I'm not the kind of person who sticks around, and it's better this way. For both of us.

The rest of the day passes in a blur of awkward avoidance. I spend most of it in my room, packing my things and trying not to think about how Ben's face looked this morning when I snapped at him. I venture out briefly for lunch, but Ben's nowhere to be seen, and I feel both relieved and disappointed.

I run into Darlene, the ever-cheerful waitress, who chats with me about her plans for the upcoming town caroling night. I nod along, offering noncommittal responses and smiling when necessary, but my mind is elsewhere. This place has been a strange kind of refuge, even if I didn't ask for it. But now it's time to go. No attachments, no regrets. That's the rule.

By late afternoon, I've run out of excuses to hide. I find myself wandering through the town square, watching as the villagers hang new decorations and prepare for yet another holiday event. It's busy, bright, and everything I once found irritatingly festive now feels almost comforting. Almost.

I spot Ben across the square, talking to a couple of local kids who are excitedly showing off their new sleds. He's smiling, but there's a heaviness in his shoulders that I can't ignore. I think about going over, saying something, but I can't seem to make my feet move. I've already made this hard enough. There's no point in dragging it out.

Instead, I turn away, letting the cold air sting my cheeks as I make my way back to the inn.

As night falls, I find myself sitting on the windowsill in my room, staring out at the village below. The square is lit up, the bonfire still crackling from last night, and a few stragglers are gathered around, sharing quiet conversations under the glow of twinkling lights. It's a scene straight out of a Christmas movie, the kind I've always hated for being too perfect, too unrealistic.

But tonight, it just feels… sad. I should be happy that I'm leaving, that I'm getting away from all this holiday cheer that's never been my thing. But instead, all I feel is this gnawing sense of loss, like I'm walking away from something important.

My phone buzzes with the bus ticket reminder, jolting me out of my thoughts. I glance at the screen, the cold, hard confirmation staring back at me. Tomorrow morning, I'll be gone. It's what I wanted. So why does it feel like I'm making a huge mistake?

There's a knock at my door, and I freeze, heart skipping a beat. I know it's Ben before I even open it. He stands there, hands shoved in his pockets, looking both hopeful and unsure.

"Hey," he says softly, his eyes searching mine. "I didn't see you much today. You okay?"

I nod, swallowing the lump in my throat. "Yeah, just… had some things to take care of."

He hesitates, and I can tell he's trying to figure out what to say. "Zoe, about this morning; I didn't mean to push. I just… I don't know, I care about you, and I don't want you to feel like you have to keep running."

His words hit me like a punch to the gut, and I feel my resolve crumbling. I want to tell him about the bus, about how I'm planning to leave, but the words stick in my throat. Instead, I just smile, a sad, forced thing that doesn't reach my eyes.

"It's fine, Ben. Really," I say, trying to sound reassuring. "I'm just figuring things out."

He nods, but I can see the hurt he's trying to hide. "Yeah. I get it."

We stand there for a moment, the silence thick and heavy between us. I wish I could say something to make it better, but I'm not sure there's anything left to say.

"Goodnight, Zoe," he finally says, his voice barely a whisper.

"Goodnight, Ben," I reply, and as he walks away, I feel the weight of my decision settle in, heavy and unyielding.

Tomorrow, I'll be gone. But tonight, I let myself watch the lights of Evergreen one last time, wondering what might have been if I'd let myself stay just a little longer.

Chapter 7

Christmas Tree Catastrophe

I wake up before dawn, my heart racing and my mind set on one thing: getting out of this town. My clothes feel stiff as I pull them on in the dim light of my room, the inn's creaky floorboards groaning under my weight. The knot in my stomach tightens as I look at my packed suitcase, waiting by the door like it's as eager to leave as I am. My bus ticket is saved on my phone, a small screen of salvation that promises an escape from Evergreen and everything that comes with it; Christmas, emotions, Ben.

I take a last look around the room, at the cozy bed I won't miss and the window that looks out onto the sleepy, snow-covered village. The town is still, cloaked in a fresh layer of snow that sparkles under the streetlights. The decorations twinkle, reflecting off the icy blanket, and for a split second, I wonder if I'm really doing the right thing. But the thought of staying, of letting this place get under my skin any more than it already has, feels too risky. I've been down that road before, letting myself care, letting myself get attached, and it never ends well.

I grab my bag, double-check my phone, and quietly make my way down the inn's staircase. The lobby is empty, dimly lit by the soft glow of a few stray Christmas lights. I don't see Ben, and I'm grateful. There's no way I could handle another conversation, another moment of him looking at me like he's seeing through all my defenses. I push the door open, feeling the icy morning air hit my face, and step outside.

Evergreen is wrapped in a winter wonderland, the kind you see in greeting cards and snow globes. The rooftops are covered in white, icicles dangle from eaves, and every tree seems to be dusted with powdered sugar. It's annoyingly beautiful, and the peacefulness of it all tugs at something deep inside me. But I force myself to keep walking, my breath coming out in small puffs as I make my way to the bus stop.

I reach the stop, my nerves jangling, only to be greeted by a handwritten sign taped to the pole: **ALL BUS SERVICES CANCELED DUE TO SEVERE WEATHER CONDITIONS.**

I stare at the sign, blinking in disbelief. Canceled? Today, of all days? I check my phone for updates, but every route out of town has been shut down because of the snowstorm that rolled in overnight. My pulse quickens, panic bubbling up as the reality of my situation sinks in. I'm stuck here, on Christmas Eve, no less, with no way out.

"Great. Just great," I mutter, kicking the snow in frustration. The universe, it seems, is determined to keep me here, forcing me to face everything I've been trying to run from. I turn back toward the inn, my feet heavy, dragging my suitcase through the snow. My grand escape has been thwarted, and now I'm back at square one, with no plan, no exit, and no idea how to deal with the mess of feelings swirling inside me.

By midday, the town square is buzzing with activity. The festival preparations are in full swing, and the village looks like it's been transformed into a scene from a Christmas movie set. There are booths selling hot cider, homemade crafts, and every kind of holiday treat imaginable. Kids dash through the snow, wearing Santa hats and scarves, their laughter ringing out like bells, while couples sip hot cocoa, sharing kisses under mistletoe. The centerpiece of it all is the town's giant Christmas tree, towering in the middle of the square, decked out in lights, ornaments, and a star that looks precariously perched at the top.

I try to keep my distance, lurking on the edges of the festival, but Evergreen has a way of drawing you in whether you want to be involved or not. I spot Ben near the cocoa stand, surrounded by villagers eager to chat with him. He's got that effortless smile on his face, the one that usually makes me feel warm and safe, but today it just feels like a reminder of how badly I've messed things up. I'm about to slip away when Darlene, the ever-enthusiastic waitress with her reindeer antlers, catches sight of me and waves me over.

"Zoe! Just the person I was looking for!" she says, grabbing my arm and dragging me toward a table covered in decorations. "We're setting up for the tree lighting ceremony tonight, and we could use your help."

I try to protest, but Darlene isn't hearing it. "Oh, come on now, don't be shy. We're all pitching in!"

I sigh, plastering on a half-hearted smile. "Sure. Why not?"

I find myself standing near the base of the giant tree, trying to look busy while mentally counting down the hours until I can try for the bus station again. The tree looms above me, a dazzling display of Christmas excess that feels completely at odds with my current mood. I'm lost in my thoughts, barely paying attention, when someone hands me a box of baubles and a ladder, asking me to hang the last of the ornaments near the top.

I eye the setup skeptically. Climbing a ladder to hang ornaments wasn't exactly on my agenda for today, but before I can say no, I'm halfway up the rickety thing, trying not to look down as I reach for the higher branches.

The festival hums around me, the air filled with the sound of carols and laughter. For a moment, as I hang the last of the decorations, I almost feel like I'm part of something; like maybe, just maybe, this isn't so bad. But that fleeting feeling vanishes the second I realize something's wrong.

The ladder wobbles beneath me, a sickening lurch that sends my stomach into free fall. I grab for the tree to steady myself, but my hand slips, pulling at a tangle of lights. The whole structure shudders, and I hear the unmistakable creak of wood and metal giving way.

"Oh no," I whisper, but it's too late. The tree tilts, swaying dangerously, and then, like a slow-motion nightmare, it begins to fall.

The tree crashes down with a deafening roar, taking with it strings of lights, ornaments, and every ounce of holiday cheer in the square. People scream and scatter, dodging branches and flying baubles as the tree collapses in a mess of tinsel and pine needles. My heart plummets as I watch it topple, unable to do anything but stare in horror.

And then, the final, heart-wrenching blow: the tree lands directly on Ben's late wife's memorial bench. The metal groans under the impact, twisting and splintering as the tree crushes the once-pristine tribute into a pile of wreckage. I hear the gasp of the crowd, feel their collective shock and dismay, and I know, without a doubt, that I've just ruined everything.

Ben reaches me first, his face stricken with a mix of shock, disbelief, and pain that I've never seen before. He looks at the tree, at the destroyed bench, and then at me, his expression breaking my heart in a way that words never could.

"Zoe," he says, his voice trembling with restrained fury. "What did you do? How could you let this happen?"

I've never heard him sound like this. Betrayed, furious, and completely blindsided. His words hit me like a slap, and I can see the sheer devastation in his eyes. It's not just about the tree or the bench; it's about everything this town stands for, everything Ben's been trying to hold onto. I want to shrink under his gaze, to disappear from the wreckage I've caused, but there's nowhere to hide from the weight of his anger.

I can barely meet his eyes, my throat tight as I struggle to find the right thing to say. "I,… I didn't mean for this to…"

But my excuses sound hollow, even to me. It doesn't matter that it was an accident. The tree is ruined, the festival is ruined, and I've destroyed the one thing that means the most to Ben. The one piece of his past that he still holds onto.

The crowd is murmuring, the mood of the festival turned dark and heavy. I can feel their stares, their judgment, and it's like a physical weight pressing down on me. Darlene rushes over, her face pale as she takes in the scene. "Oh, honey… this is a real mess."

Ben doesn't say anything else. He just turns away, his shoulders rigid, and walks off without another word. It's worse than if he'd yelled, worse than if he'd told me how badly I've messed up. His silence cuts deeper than any outburst ever could, and I'm left standing there, alone in the wreckage of my own making.

I want to fix it, to turn back time and undo what I've done, but there's no way to make it right. The festival is a disaster, Ben is hurt, and the town that had slowly begun to welcome me now looks at me like I'm the enemy, the outsider who ruined their perfect Christmas Eve.

As I stand there, surrounded by broken branches and shattered ornaments, I realize that I've made a mess of everything - again. And this time, I don't know if there's any way to put it back together.

Chapter 8

Breaking the Heart of Christmas

The silence that blankets the square is suffocating, heavy and thick, like a weight pressing down on my chest. It's the kind of silence that fills the space where joy used to be, swallowing up the carols, the laughter, and the sounds of children's excited chatter. Now, all that remains is the dull crunch of boots on snow and the faint, eerie tinkle of broken glass being swept into piles. The once-bright and cheerful square, filled with twinkling lights and festive decorations, now resembles the aftermath of a storm; chaotic, broken, and impossibly sad.

Everywhere I look, people are picking through the wreckage with careful, deliberate movements, like they're afraid to touch anything in case it shatters further. The Christmas tree lies on its side, its once-majestic branches sprawled out like the limbs of a fallen giant. Ornaments that were carefully hung just hours ago now lay in pieces, glittering shards that catch the pale winter light like cruel, mocking stars. Strands of tinsel are tangled and twisted, draped limply across the square as if even they have given up. But the real damage isn't in the scattered debris, it's in the faces of the people around me.

The villagers, who had once greeted me with warmth and generosity, now glare at me with a mixture of anger, disappointment, and something far worse: betrayal. Their expressions cut through me like knives, each one sharper than the last. I can feel their judgment, heavy and palpable, pressing in on all sides, as if they're waiting for me to break under the weight of it. And I just might. I want to look away, to escape their piercing stares, but it's impossible. There's nowhere to hide from the mess I've made.

The whispers start as soft murmurs, barely audible at first, but they grow louder with each passing second, rippling through the crowd like a current of disapproval that's impossible to ignore.

"Did you see what she did? Who climbs a tree during a festival?"

"How could she be so careless? She's been nothing but trouble since she got here."

"This was supposed to be the highlight of the night. She's ruined everything."

Their words sting, each one a fresh wound that tears at my already frayed nerves. I flinch with every accusation, each sharp comment sinking in deeper, the weight of their collective disappointment threatening to crush me. My hands tremble at my sides, and I want to speak, to defend myself, but my throat is tight, strangled by guilt and shame that feel like they're suffocating me from the inside out. I can't even form a coherent sentence, let alone explain that this was never my intention. But intentions don't matter now. All that matters is what I've done.

My gaze drifts, and I spot Ben standing a few feet away, still as a statue amidst the swirling chaos. He looks like he's been sucker-punched, his face drained of color, eyes wide with disbelief. There's anger there, too. Hot and simmering just beneath the surface. But what hurts the most is the hurt, the sense of betrayal that flickers across his features. He trusted me, believed that I was here for more than just passing through, and now he's staring at me like he doesn't recognize the person standing before him. I feel sick, my stomach twisting into knots. I've hurt him, and I don't know how to make it right.

Before I can even think of what to say, Darlene storms toward me, her usually cheerful face twisted with exasperation and something that looks like heartbreak. She's clutching an ornament in her hand; an angel that used to hang at the top of the tree, its delicate wings now snapped off, the pieces dangling by a thin thread. The sight of it is like a punch to the gut, a physical manifestation of all the damage I've caused in just a few short moments.

"Zoe," Darlene says, and her voice is thick with restrained emotion, teetering on the edge of breaking. "What were you thinking? You were supposed to help, not… not this." She gestures broadly at the fallen tree, the scattered decorations, the ruined bench - Ben's late wife's bench, the one that meant everything to him. The bench that's now bent and broken beneath the weight of my recklessness.

I swallow hard, my mouth dry, panic rising in my throat like bile. "Darlene, I'm sorry," I manage to say, my voice barely more than a whisper. "It was an accident! I was just trying to fix the lights. I never meant for this to happen."

Darlene shakes her head, her eyes shining with unshed tears, her frustration bubbling over. "Fix them?" she repeats, her voice rising, tinged with disbelief. "Zoe, you've gone and broken the heart of this festival! This tree isn't just a decoration; it's a symbol of this town, of everything we've worked so hard to build. And that bench…" Her voice catches, and she presses a hand to her chest as if trying to steady herself. "That bench was for Sarah, Ben's wife. It was supposed to be a place where we could all remember her. You can't just… this was supposed to be a good day, Zoe. A day of joy."

Her words are like a punch to the stomach, knocking the wind out of me. I feel the weight of what she's saying, every syllable sinking in and pulling me deeper into my own sense of guilt. This wasn't just some random tree or some meaningless bench. They were touchstones of this community, of their memories, their grief, their joy. And now, because of me, those touchstones lie in ruins.

I can't hold back the tears any longer. They spill down my cheeks, hot and fast, blurring my vision as I stare at the mess I've made. I try to say something, anything to make this right, but my voice cracks, and all that comes out is a strangled sob. I've never felt more like an outsider, more like the wrecking ball I've spent my whole life pretending I'm not.

"I'm sorry," I whisper again, but it sounds so small, so insignificant against the enormity of what I've done. I'm not sure if Darlene hears me, or if she even cares. The damage is done, and no apology can piece the fallen tree back together or mend the broken bench that meant so much to Ben. I've taken something beautiful and turned it into a scene of devastation, and there's no way to take it back.

The villagers keep their distance, but their disappointment is palpable, hanging in the air like a storm cloud ready to burst. I look around at their faces, at the mess of shattered ornaments and toppled decorations, and all I can think is how badly I've let them down. This town opened its arms to me, and I've repaid them with nothing but heartache.

I glance back at Ben, but he doesn't move, doesn't speak. He just watches, his expression carved from stone, and it's that silence - his silence - that hurts the most.

My chest tightens as Darlene's words sink in. I can feel the weight of her disappointment, the sting of everyone's disapproval, and it's like I'm drowning in it. My mouth opens to respond, to apologize, but nothing comes out. I'm trapped in the wreckage of my own making, and I don't know how to claw my way out.

But before I can even try to find my voice, a new noise breaks through the tension; a commotion at the edge of the square. Heads turn, and I follow their gaze, my heart sinking as I spot a group of strangers moving toward us, dressed in bright winter gear that screams "tourists." Cameras dangle from their necks, and they're all chattering excitedly, eyes wide with the kind of morbid fascination reserved for roadside accidents and reality TV.

They're not from Evergreen. They don't belong here. And the realization hits me like a punch to the gut: they're my blog readers. The ones who've been eating up my sarcastic posts about this place, laughing along with every snarky comment I've made about the town and its over-the-top Christmas spirit. And now, they're here, in the flesh, drawn in by my bitterness like moths to a flame.

My stomach churns as the crowd of readers pushes closer, oblivious to the tension swirling around them. They're smiling, snapping photos of the fallen tree, the broken ornaments, the chaos that's spread across the square like a stain. To them, this is just another quirky anecdote in a long line of Zoe's misadventures, something to share on social media with a cheeky caption and a laughing emoji. But to me, and to everyone else here, it's a nightmare made real.

"Oh my gosh, Zoe!" A woman with bright red earmuffs and a fur-lined coat breaks away from the group, waving at me like I'm a long-lost friend or some kind of celebrity. Her smile is blinding, full of excitement, and completely out of place in this sea of anger and hurt. "I can't believe it's really you! We've been following your blog. This town is exactly as ridiculous as you said!"

Her voice cuts through the air, cheerful and oblivious, and the words hit me like a splash of ice water. I feel every pair of eyes in the square swivel toward me, the villagers' confusion deepening into something sharper, something far more dangerous. For a moment, everything seems to freeze - time, sound, even my breath - and all I can hear is the rushing in my ears as panic claws its way up my throat.

The woman continues, her voice loud and carefree, completely missing the undercurrent of tension. "We just had to come see for ourselves! I mean, who knew a place like this could actually exist? It's like stepping into a Christmas movie gone wrong. So over-the-top and cheesy. Just like you said!"

She giggles, a light, airy sound that feels like nails on a chalkboard, and I flinch, feeling every ounce of goodwill I've tried to build in this town crumble into dust. The villagers are staring at me, their expressions shifting from confusion to betrayal, to outright anger. The realization is dawning on them, one by one, they're connecting the dots between my sarcastic posts and the disaster unfolding before them. To them, I'm not just the girl who accidentally ruined their festival; I'm the outsider who's been mocking them from the start, treating their cherished traditions like a joke.

I glance at Ben, hoping for some sign of understanding, but his face is stony, his eyes dark with a mix of hurt and fury. It's the kind of look that makes my heart twist in my chest, because I know that whatever fragile connection we had is splintering right in front of me. He takes a step forward, his gaze never leaving mine, and there's a tension in his posture, like he's holding back everything he wants to say.

"What is this, Zoe?" he asks, his voice low but filled with a simmering anger that I've never heard from him before. "Who are these people? Why are they here?"

I try to answer, but my words stick in my throat. I've never felt more exposed, more cornered, and I can see the lines of disappointment etched into every face around me. I've been caught, and there's no talking my way out of this.

"They're just… readers," I manage to choke out, my voice sounding hollow and weak even to my own ears. "They read my blog, and I guess they…"

Ben cuts me off, his voice rising, each word sharper than the last. "Your blog? You mean those posts where you've been making fun of us? Of this town? You've been laughing at everything we've shared with you, haven't you?"

The accusation is a punch to the gut, and I stumble back, desperate to find some way to explain. "No, it's not like that… I didn't mean for any of this to happen. I was just… venting."

"Venting?" Ben's voice is incredulous, his anger boiling over. "You've been writing about us like we're some kind of joke, and now you've brought these people here to laugh at us? At our lives?"

I try to protest, but the words are coming too fast, the panic too overwhelming. "I didn't bring them here! I was just writing, and I didn't think…"

"You didn't think at all!" Ben shouts, and the rawness in his voice stops me cold. "We trusted you, Zoe. I trusted you. And all this time, you've been mocking us behind our backs."

The crowd is closing in, the villagers' whispers growing louder, their anger feeding off Ben's words. I look around, desperate for an ally, but all I see are accusing eyes, frowns, and the crushing realization that I've lost whatever place I'd begun to carve out here. The woman with the red earmuffs is still grinning, snapping photos of the mess, completely unaware of the damage she's helping to expose. To her, this is just a funny story, a quirky little moment in an otherwise mundane holiday. But to me, it's everything falling apart.

I glance back at Ben, but he's already turning away, his expression hardening as he puts distance between us. The hurt in his eyes is the final blow, and I feel my knees weaken, my composure hanging by a thread. He doesn't say another word, just walks away, leaving me standing in the middle of the square, surrounded by the wreckage I've created.

It's like every sarcastic comment, every snide remark I've ever made has come back to haunt me in the worst possible way. The square falls silent, and suddenly it's just me, standing in front of everyone, my rawest, most painful truths spilling out in a messy, tangled heap. I can see the confusion in their eyes, the judgment, but I can't stop the flood of words now. They've been buried for too long, clawing their way to the surface, and all I can do is let them out.

"I hate Christmas because it's never been what it's supposed to be," I confess, my voice shaking with years of bitterness and hurt. "My dad left on Christmas morning when I was nine. He just packed his bags and walked out without a word. Every year after that, it was just me and my mom, pretending to be okay while the rest of the world celebrated. Christmas isn't joy and love and family. It's a reminder of everything I lost."

I choke on the tears, my voice cracking as I finally say the things I've never dared to say. "I use sarcasm because it's easier than letting myself feel anything real. It's easier than getting hurt. I push people away because I'm scared! Scared of caring, scared of losing, scared of messing up something good because I don't know how to be part of it."

Ben turns around after he hears my words. His face softens, but the hurt doesn't disappear; it lingers, etched into every line and wrinkle, the pain still fresh and raw. "Zoe, I'm sorry," he says quietly, his voice filled with a mix of empathy and sadness. "I didn't know. But that doesn't make this okay."

I nod, my heart aching, knowing that he's right. No amount of explanation can undo what I've done. "I know," I whisper, my voice barely audible over the soft hum of the wind. "I know it doesn't. But I'm trying, Ben. I'm trying so hard, and I don't know how to fix this. I don't know how to be part of something good without ruining it."

Ben's eyes search mine, as if he's trying to find the person he thought I was, but all he sees now is the mess I've made. He looks away, his shoulders slumping with the weight of it all, and I can feel the distance growing between us, widening like a chasm that I can't cross. "I need time," he says finally, his voice barely above a whisper. "I can't deal with this right now."

I watch helplessly as he turns and walks away, every step he takes feeling like another crack in my already shattered heart. I want to call out to him, to beg him to understand, but the words won't come. I've lost him, and it's my fault. No amount of apologies can change that.

The villagers begin to disperse, their faces filled with a mix of anger, pity, and disappointment. My readers linger awkwardly, their excitement drained, replaced by a heavy sense of unease. One of them, a young woman with bright blue earmuffs and an apologetic smile, steps forward, her voice timid. "I'm sorry, Zoe. We didn't mean to cause any trouble. We just… thought it would be fun to see the town you wrote about."

I nod, but it feels empty. Everything feels empty. "It's not your fault," I whisper, my voice hollow. "It's mine. All of it."

They back away, giving me space, and I sink down onto a nearby bench, feeling the weight of everything I've done settle over me like a heavy, suffocating blanket. I bury my face in my hands, the tears coming harder, burning against the cold, and all I can think is how badly I've messed up. I thought I was protecting myself by keeping everyone at a distance, but now I've pushed away the one place, the one person, that made me feel seen.

As the snow falls softly around me, each delicate flake glistening like tiny, fleeting hopes, I feel the weight of everything I've confessed settle over me. I've said my truth, laid it all bare for Ben and the entire town to see, but it still feels like there's a mountain left to climb. I close my eyes, fighting the tears that won't stop coming, and in a moment of quiet desperation, I whisper a silent plea to the universe, maybe even to the Christmas spirit I've never believed in.

"Please," I think, my heart aching with every beat. "Give me a sign, an idea, anything. I need a Christmas miracle to turn this around. Not for me, but for everyone I've let down."

I lift my head, staring at the snow-covered square that should have been filled with joy and laughter, and all I can do is hope - hope for a spark of inspiration, a way to fix this, something that can bring back the light I've snuffed out. I need a miracle, and I need it now.

Chapter 9

Glitter, Hope, and Holiday Magic

I sit on the cold bench, my breath puffing out in clouds that disappear into the freezing air, my fingers numb from the cold. Everything around me feels like a slow-motion scene from a movie I never wanted to star in; the fallen tree, the broken bench, the disappointed faces of the villagers. The weight of my mistakes presses down on me, and for a moment, I want to disappear into the snow, let it cover me until no one remembers I was ever here. But the gentle hum of Christmas carols that still play faintly from a distant speaker and the soft glow of twinkling lights buried under the snow remind me that it's not over. Christmas isn't over.

The thought strikes me like a sudden burst of warmth; a tiny spark of hope in the freezing darkness. I look around at the chaos, at the toppled tree lying on its side like a defeated soldier, and the idea begins to grow. I can't undo what I've done, but maybe, just maybe, I can fix it. It's not too late. I've been running from Christmas my whole life, but maybe this is my chance to finally get it right.

I stand up, brushing the snow from my jeans, determination rising inside me. I've spent my whole life running from every mess I've made, but this time, I won't. I won't let Christmas end like this; not for me, and not for Evergreen.

I take a deep breath and pull out my phone. My hands shake, partly from the cold and partly from the fear of what I'm about to do. I open my blog and stare at the blank screen, feeling the weight of my readers' expectations. These are the people I've entertained with my sarcasm and snark, the ones who've laughed at my misadventures and shared in my cynicism. They came here because of me, and now, I need them more than ever.

I start typing, the words spilling out faster than I can think.

"*To my readers,*" I begin, my fingers trembling as they fly over the keyboard, each keystroke feeling like a desperate plea. "*I've been wrong. So wrong. About Christmas, about this town, and about the people who live here. I came to Evergreen expecting to hate everything about it—the over-the-top decorations, the relentless cheer, the sense of belonging that always felt just out of reach for someone like me. I mocked it all because it was easier than admitting that maybe, just maybe, I wanted to be a part of it. But I've been hiding behind my sarcasm and my walls for so long that I forgot how to just… be. Be honest. Be kind. Be open. And now, I've made a mess that I can't fix alone.*"

I pause, swallowing hard as I feel the sting of tears threatening to spill again, but I push on, knowing that this moment demands every ounce of honesty I have left.

"*I've let you all down,*" I type, my chest tightening with the weight of my own words. "*I made jokes at the expense of something real, something beautiful, and I've hurt people who didn't deserve it. I turned this town into a punchline, and in doing so, I forgot what it means to let yourself feel the magic of this time of year. I lost sight of what I was really looking for: connection, hope, and maybe even a little bit of Christmas spirit. And now, standing here in the middle of the wreckage I've caused, I'm asking—no, I'm begging—you to forgive me."*

I blink back the tears, my vision blurring as I pour my heart into the post, knowing that this is my last chance to turn things around.

"Christmas isn't over yet," I continue, my words spilling out faster now, tinged with the desperation I've been trying to keep at bay. *"There's still time to make things right. But I can't do it alone. I need your help to fix what I've broken. I need your spirit, your kindness, your traditions, your everything. If you're still here, if you've got even a shred of holiday magic left, meet me at the square. Let's pick up the pieces. Let's get the tree back up, and let's create something beautiful out of this mess together. I know I don't deserve it, but I'm asking anyway. Please help me bring Christmas back to Evergreen. Help me show this town that it's not too late for a miracle."*

I take a deep breath, my fingers hovering over the "post" button, fear and hope battling in my chest. I've never been this vulnerable, this raw, and as I press "post," I feel like I'm standing on the edge of a cliff, waiting to see if anyone will catch me.

I look up at the fallen tree, the ruined decorations, and I brace myself for the worst. Maybe no one will come. Maybe this is the moment they all realize I'm not worth the trouble.

But then, one by one, I see them. My readers, dressed in bright coats and scarves, slowly making their way toward me. They look uncertain at first, but there's something else in their eyes, too; hope, maybe, or the faintest flicker of excitement. They're here, and they're ready to help.

A woman in a yellow coat with a camera slung around her neck steps forward, offering me a tentative smile. "So, what's the plan, Zoe?"

I blink back tears, overwhelmed by the unexpected support. "We fix this," I say, my voice firm. "We clean up this mess, we put the tree back up, and we bring Christmas back to Evergreen."

They nod, and before I know it, everyone is in motion. It's like a switch has been flipped, a new energy buzzing in the air as my readers start picking up the scattered ornaments, the broken lights, and the crushed decorations. I grab a broom and start sweeping up the shattered glass, and soon, others join in, their laughter and chatter filling the square once again.

I can't believe it. It's actually working. We're doing it.

Someone connects a speaker, and instead of my usual rock music, the soft, familiar strains of classic Christmas carols fill the air. "Jingle Bells" kicks off, and I can't help but smile as people start to hum along, the festive spirit creeping back into the town. The music echoes down the streets, and before long, villagers who had been on their way home begin to trickle back, drawn by the sounds of laughter and the sight of the tree being reborn.

As we work, people begin to share their own ideas, their own little pieces of Christmas magic. A man with a bushy beard and a Santa hat suggests that we string popcorn garlands to replace the tinsel that was ruined. A group of teenagers start crafting makeshift ornaments out of whatever they can find; pinecones, sticks, even soda cans that they paint and sprinkle with glitter until they shimmer in the dim light.

"Let's add some of our traditions, too," one of the women says, holding up a handful of cinnamon sticks tied with red ribbon. "This is how we decorate back home. It'll make everything smell like Christmas."

The crowd agrees, and soon, they're hanging cinnamon sticks, dried oranges, and handmade paper snowflakes all over the tree. It's far from perfect, but it's something. It's messy, and it's beautiful, and it's exactly what this moment needs. I step back, wiping my brow and taking it all in. The tree isn't flawless anymore; it's patched together with bits of whatever we could find, but it's glowing with life. It's glowing with heart.

Darlene, who had been glaring at me not long ago, returns with her arms full of cookies and hot cocoa. "Well, look at that," she says, handing out steaming cups to anyone who passes by. "We've got ourselves a Christmas miracle, don't we?"

I laugh, more out of relief than anything else. "Yeah, I guess we do."

Children rush up to the tree, eager to add their own touches, hanging ornaments they've found in their homes or crafting new ones out of buttons, fabric scraps, and anything they can get their hands on. A little boy places a lopsided star at the top, and everyone cheers as it lights up. It's crooked, but it's perfect.

I can hardly believe it. The square that had felt so broken just moments ago is alive again, buzzing with activity and joy. The villagers are back, their initial anger replaced by a hesitant sense of hope, and my readers are mingling with them, sharing stories and traditions, making this moment feel like a celebration of everyone's different versions of Christmas.

But even in the midst of this small, beautiful miracle, my eyes keep drifting back to the bench; the one thing I can't seem to fix with glitter and garlands. It sits beneath the newly raised tree, its metal frame twisted, its wood splintered, a painful reminder of everything I've broken that can't be mended with a quick patch job. The bench meant so much to Ben, a quiet tribute to Sarah that had given comfort to more than just him; it had become a part of this town's fabric, a place where people could sit, remember, and feel connected to someone they loved.

I walk over to it, the joyful sounds of the square fading into the background. I run my fingers over the jagged edge, feeling the weight of what it represents; memories, loss, love. It's not just a bench; it's a piece of Sarah's legacy, something that can't be replaced by another decoration or a hastily crafted ornament.

My chest tightens as I stare at it, my mind racing for a solution, a way to make this right. I can fix a tree, I can clean up a mess, but how do you fix something that holds so much meaning? How do you repair something that was a symbol of a life, of a love story cut short?

I kneel beside the bench, my fingers tracing the worn wood, feeling the rough, splintered edges beneath my touch. Each crack and scratch tells a story, and I can't help but feel the weight of Sarah's memory pressing down on me, heavy and unyielding. Lost in thought, I barely notice the quiet shuffle of footsteps behind me until a deep, gravelly voice breaks the silence.

"It's a special bench, you know," says Bob, the gruff but kind-hearted mechanic who's been working on Rusty. He's standing just behind me, his hands tucked into the pockets of his worn coat, looking at the bench with a mix of sadness and reverence. "Just because something breaks doesn't mean it's worthless. The act of repair is where the true love lies."

His words hit me hard, and I feel a lump forming in my throat. I glance up at Bob, his weathered face softened by the glow of the Christmas lights. "I messed it up," I whisper, my voice thick with regret. "I don't know how to fix something like this. I wish I could… I wish I could bring it back the way it was."

Bob crouches down beside me, his gaze steady and understanding. "You know, Sarah was the kind of person who believed in fixing things, not just throwing them away when they broke. She'd see this as a chance to make it better than before, not just put it back the way it was."

I swallow hard, feeling the sting of tears again. "I want to fix it, but I don't have the skills or the tools. I wouldn't even know where to start."

Bob smiles, a slow, reassuring grin that reaches his eyes. "Well, lucky for you, I've got both. I can fix it. It'll take some time, but I know how to make it right."

I blink, caught off guard by his kindness. For a moment, I'm speechless, overwhelmed by the generosity of this man who's already done so much for me. Without thinking, I throw my arms around him, pulling him into a tight hug. "Thank you," I murmur, my voice choked with gratitude. "Thank you so much."

Bob chuckles, patting my back awkwardly before stepping away. "You've done good here, Zoe. Don't let this one thing eat at you. We all mess up. What matters is how we fix it." He pauses for a moment, inspecting the bench with a practiced eye, then adds casually, "Oh, and by the way, your car's ready for pickup whenever you're set. Rusty's all patched up." He digs into his coat pocket, fishing around for a moment before pulling out my car keys. With a small smile, he holds them out to me.

I blink, caught off guard by his matter-of-fact tone. My heart swells with gratitude for this man who's already done so much more than just fix a broken car. "Thank you, Bob," I say, my voice catching. "Really, thank you for everything."

I nod, my heart full as I watch Bob carefully assess the bench, his fingers running over the damaged wood with the kind of reverence only someone who understands loss could have. But as I stand up, wiping the tears from my cheeks, my gaze drifts to the edge of the square where Ben is standing, half-hidden in the shadows, watching us. His face is unreadable, a mix of lingering disappointment and something else; something softer, though still distant.

Our eyes meet, and for a brief second, it feels like the entire chaotic square falls away. I don't know if he's ready to forgive me, but seeing him there, watching quietly, fills me with a sliver of hope. I offer a small, tentative smile, hoping he can see that I'm trying, that I'm not giving up on this town, or on him.

Ben doesn't move, doesn't say a word, but he doesn't look away either. It's not the reunion I hoped for, but it's a start, and for now, that's enough. As Bob sets to work, I turn back to the square, determined to finish what I've started. There's still more to be done, and Christmas isn't over yet.

Chapter 10

A Place to Heal

The soft light of Christmas morning filters through the curtains, casting a gentle glow across my room. For the first time in a long time, I wake up with a sense of peace. Last night, we didn't just save a Christmas tree, we saved something far more important. The square that had felt broken and hopeless had been transformed into a glittering, chaotic celebration of everyone's spirit, their willingness to forgive, and their desire to come together despite everything. The villagers, my readers, and I had pulled off what felt like a Christmas miracle, and it was beautiful.

I stretch in bed, feeling a warmth that has nothing to do with the heater humming gently in the corner. My phone buzzes on the nightstand, and I reach for it, half-expecting a flurry of messages or comments from my readers. Instead, there's a notification from the delivery app I used late last night. I grin, remembering my frantic order placed in the early hours of the morning when I couldn't sleep.

"I love overnight delivery," I mumble to myself with a smirk. "They're like my own personal Santa Claus on Christmas morning."

I throw on my coat, not bothering to change out of my pajamas, and head downstairs. The inn is quiet, the peaceful kind of silence that only a holiday morning can bring. As I push open the front door, I spot the delivery guy standing by his truck, a package in hand, and I feel a rush of excitement. He waves when he sees me, and I hurry over, my breath puffing out in the crisp air.

"Merry Christmas!" he says cheerfully, handing me the package.

"Merry Christmas," I reply, taking the box with a grateful smile. The package is heavier than I expected, but the weight feels good, it's the weight of a promise, a chance to make things right. I thank the driver, tucking the box under my arm as I head back inside, a plan already forming in my mind.

But first, there's one more thing I need. I check the time; it's still early, but I know just the place that will be open. The gas station at the edge of town is the only spot in Evergreen that doesn't close for Christmas, and it's exactly where I'm headed.

I trudge through the snow, shivering a little as I make my way inside. The fluorescent lights buzz overhead, illuminating aisles filled with snacks, coffee, and an odd assortment of last-minute gifts. But I'm not here for any of that. I make a beeline for the small gardening section tucked in the back—a weirdly out-of-place display of plantable flowers, a tiny potted tree, and a row of brightly colored seed packets.

I grab as many plants as I can carry, my arms overflowing with poinsettias, small evergreens, and any other flowers I can find. I even manage to snag a small bag of bulbs and a rusty shovel propped up against the wall. My fingers are practically numb from the cold, and I keep dropping things as I awkwardly fumble my way toward the counter.

Just as I'm trying to balance the last pot on top of my pile, two elderly women approach, eyeing my clumsy struggle with amused smiles. One of them, dressed in a red coat with a green knitted scarf, chuckles and reaches out to steady the tree I'm about to drop for the third time.

"Looks like you've got your hands full there, dear," she says warmly. "Need a hand?"

"Yes, please," I laugh, feeling a little breathless. "I'm trying to make a Christmas miracle, and I think I'm one clumsy step away from making a Christmas disaster."

The women help me gather the plants and carry them to the counter, chatting about their holiday plans as we go. It's a simple kindness, but it feels like magic; the kind that's been the heart of Evergreen, ever since I stepped foot in it. We head out of the store, and I thank them profusely as they help load everything into my arms.

"You're doing something good, I can tell," one of them says with a knowing smile. "Keep at it."

With their encouragement, I head back toward Bob's garage, struggling to keep hold of everything as I make my way through the snow. By the time I arrive, my arms are shaking, and I've dropped at least three plants along the way, but I make it, panting and determined.

As I approach, I see Bob already hard at work on the bench, a couple of villagers gathered around him, their breath steaming in the cold as they help sand down the splintered wood and polish the metal frame. It's a quiet, diligent effort, everyone working together to restore the bench that means so much to this town.

Bob looks up as I arrive, his eyes crinkling into a smile when he sees the assortment of plants and the little tree I'm struggling to keep upright. "Looks like you've been busy," he says, putting down his tools.

"Figured Sarah deserved something beautiful," I say, setting everything down and wiping the sweat from my brow despite the chill. "I want to make a little garden around the bench. A place people can come and sit, think, remember."

Bob nods, his expression softening. "That's a fine idea, Zoe. She would have loved that."

We get to work, the villagers quickly joining in to help clear a space in the snow. Some bring spades and trowels, others their bare hands, working together to dig out a small plot at the heart of the square. It's backbreaking and messy, but no one complains. We're all in it together, bound by this unspoken desire to make something beautiful from what was broken.

I plant each flower with care, imagining the burst of color that will come in the spring, and dig a spot for the small tree, positioning it just to the right of the bench. It's not perfect, there's still snow everywhere, and some of the plants look a little worse for wear, but it's a start. A fresh beginning for a place that means so much to so many.

As we finish planting, Bob and a few others carefully lift the newly restored bench and carry it to its spot, placing it gently in the middle of the garden we've created. It's beautiful, simple, heartfelt, and full of life. The perfect tribute to Sarah.

Just as we're admiring our work, I see Ben lingering at the edge of the square again. He's been watching, his expression unreadable, and for a moment, my heart races. I take a deep breath, clutching the beautifully wrapped box in my hands, and make my way over to him.

"Hey," I say softly, my voice trembling just a little as I hand him the box. "I, um, got something for the bench. For Sarah."

Ben looks at me, then down at the box, his eyes flickering with curiosity and a hint of apprehension. He opens it slowly, carefully peeling back the wrapping to reveal a small, elegant plaque inside. His breath catches as he reads the inscription:

"In loving memory of Sarah. A place for quiet moments, where broken hearts find comfort, and memories bloom. Forever cherished, forever loved."

Ben's eyes glisten as he runs his fingers over the words, his emotions flickering across his face like shadows. For a moment, he's silent, just holding the plaque as if it's the most precious thing in the world. Then he looks at me, his expression a mix of gratitude and lingering sadness.

"Thank you," he says, his voice thick with emotion. "This… this means a lot."

I swallow hard, feeling tears prick at the corners of my eyes. "I'm so sorry, Ben. For everything. I didn't mean to hurt you, or Sarah's memory. I've spent so much of my life pushing people away because I'm scared of messing things up, but you… you've shown me what it means to belong. I want to make it right. I want to be part of this place."

Ben nods, his eyes meeting mine with a softness I haven't seen in days. "You already are, Zoe. More than you know."

He steps forward, his hand resting on the bench, and together we attach the plaque, securing it in place with the kind of care that makes my heart swell. As we finish, a cheer rises up from the villagers around us, the sound of clapping, laughter, and joy filling the square.

Ben turns to me, a tear finally slipping down his cheek. "I forgive you, Zoe. And thank you for giving this bench a new beginning."

I smile, the warmth of his words wrapping around me like a comforting embrace. "Merry Christmas, Ben," I whisper, feeling the weight of the past few days lift from my shoulders. "And thank you for giving me one, too."

We stand there, side by side, watching as the villagers gather around the garden, celebrating this new addition to their town, a place of memories, hope, and second chances. It's not just a bench anymore; it's a symbol of everything we've gone through and everything we've overcome.

As the snow begins to fall again, blanketing the square in a fresh layer of white, I finally feel at peace. We've created something beautiful out of the mess, and for the first time in my life, I'm exactly where I want to be.

Chapter 11

Final Blog Post:

Finding Christmas in Evergreen

Post Title:

Finding Christmas in Evergreen: A Journey of the Grinch's sarcastic, over-caffeinated cousin to Grateful Evergreen Resident

I've spent most of my life running from Christmas, dodging holiday cheer like it was an annoying neighbor who wouldn't stop knocking at my door. I was the self-proclaimed Grinch's over-caffeinated cousin, the queen of sarcasm, and the first to roll my eyes at the sight of twinkling lights and holiday sales. To me, Christmas was just another day—a reminder of everything that was broken, messy, and imperfect in my life.

But then, I stumbled into Evergreen. I thought it would be another blip on my travel radar, another quaint town I'd poke fun at and leave behind without a second thought. But Evergreen had other plans. This place didn't just open its doors to me; it opened my heart, bit by bit, even when I didn't want it to.

I've seen this town at its best and its worst. I watched it fall apart, and then, with the help of a few incredible people (including some of you who came all the way here because of my blog!), I got to see it come back to life. We didn't just put up a tree or hang some lights—we created something magical together. We took what was broken and made it beautiful again, and in doing so, I found something I didn't even know I was looking for: a sense of belonging.

Evergreen is the kind of place that makes you believe in second chances, in forgiveness, and in the quiet power of community. It's a town that embraces its flaws, its cracks, and its imperfections, and turns them into something worth celebrating. It's a place where people don't just sit by and watch things fall apart—they come together, roll up their sleeves, and fix it, making it better than before.

Yesterday, I watched as villagers and strangers turned a broken square into a wonderland of laughter, kindness, and shared traditions. I watched as a simple bench, dedicated to someone deeply loved and dearly missed, was restored with more care and love than I've ever seen. And I watched Ben, who had every right to shut me out, stand by and give me the gift of forgiveness.

Evergreen has taught me that sometimes the things that break are the things that bring us together. That a fallen tree isn't the end of a story, but the beginning of something new. That even the most stubborn, sarcastic Grinch can find her heart in a little town with big spirit.

So here I am, sitting on a freshly restored bench in the middle of a tiny garden, surrounded by people who have become more than just characters in my blog. They've become friends, a community, a family. And for the first time in a long time, I'm not running away. I'm staying right here, in Evergreen, where Christmas is more than just a holiday—it's a feeling, a connection, and a reminder that no matter how far we stray, there's always a way back.

From the bottom of my not-so-Grinchy heart, thank you for being part of this journey with me. Whether you were here in person, following along from afar, or just stopping by for a bit of holiday cheer, you've helped make this Christmas one I'll never forget. I've found my place, my people, and a little bit of magic I didn't even know I needed.

Merry Christmas from Evergreen. And who knows? Maybe next year, you'll find yourself here, too.

With love,
Zoe

I hit "post" and close my laptop, feeling a sense of peace settle over me like the soft, falling snow. For the first time in years, I'm not thinking about where I'm going next or what adventure I'll chase after. I'm right where I want to be.

I look over at Ben, sitting beside me on the bench, his arm casually draped over the back as he watches the village wake up. There's a quiet between us, but it's the kind that feels full, not empty. The kind that speaks of understanding, forgiveness, and something unspoken that still feels new and hopeful.

"This turned out pretty great," Ben says softly, glancing over at the garden blooming with the promise of spring, despite the blanket of snow. "Sarah would've loved it."

I smile, my heart warm as I nod.

Ben looks at me, and for a moment, the world feels still, as if holding its breath in the quiet calm of Christmas morning. "I'm glad you're staying," he says, his voice sincere, tinged with the soft vulnerability that has made me fall for this town and the people in it.

"Me too," I whisper, my fingers brushing his as they rest on the bench between us. We sit there, side by side, watching as the villagers gather, laughter mingling with the sound of carols playing faintly in the background. There's a peace that settles over everything, a quiet contentment that wraps around us like a warm embrace.

The snow continues to fall gently, each flake landing softly, adding to the fresh white blanket that covers the town. It's not just snow, it's a clean slate, a new beginning, and a reminder that even the coldest days can hold the promise of something beautiful.

As the morning unfolds, I find myself thinking that maybe, just maybe, I've found my own little Christmas miracle. Not in perfect decorations or planned festivities, but in the messy, unpredictable moments that make life worth living. In the cracks that let the light in, in the hearts that choose to forgive, and in the town that welcomed me home.

Evergreen isn't just a place on a map anymore, it's a part of me. And as I sit there, my shoulder brushing against Ben's, I know one thing for sure: this is just the beginning of something truly wonderful.

We watch the world wake up together, wrapped in the warmth of the new day, ready to embrace wherever this journey leads.